Beauty and the Beast

Retold by Richard Northcott

Illustrated by Catty Flores

Play Station 1

 1 Look and write. Then listen and check.

castle
forest
happy
monster
sad
story
woman

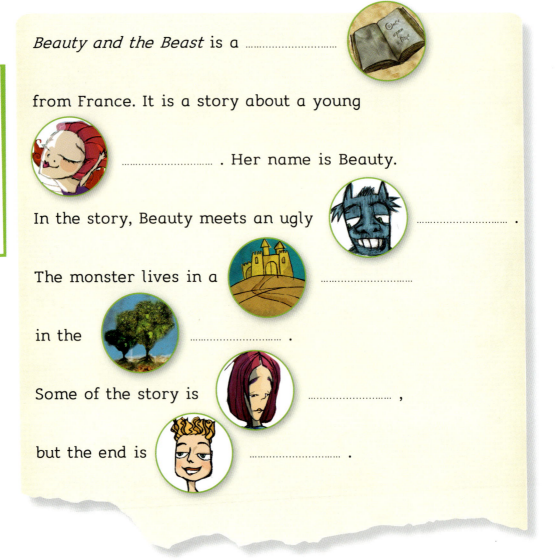

Beauty and the Beast is a ....

from France. It is a story about a young

.... Her name is Beauty.

In the story, Beauty meets an ugly ....

The monster lives in a ....

in the ....

Some of the story is .... ,

but the end is ....

 2 Do you know this story? Tell a friend.

 3 Find six words for family members. Write the words.

....

....

 4 Listen and complete. Use the words from Exercise **3**.

This is Beauty's ....
He has got three .... s.
He hasn't got any .... s.

Beauty

These are Beauty's .... s.
Beauty hasn't got any .... s.

This is Beauty.
She lives with her father.
She hasn't got a ....

Play Station 1

5 Look and match.

6 Look and ask a friend.

Who is tired?

7 Now mime and ask. What am I?

 8 Look, read and match. Then listen and check.

A I was in a forest.
I came to a castle.

C Last night in bed,
I had a dream.

E Then I heard
something behind me.

B I saw a hand on my
shoulder.

D Then I woke up.

F In the castle,
I found an old book.

 9 Write. Use the words in green from Exercise **8**.

TODAY	come	find	have	hear	see	wake up
YESTERDAY						

5

A man lived in a big house with his three daughters. The two older daughters had lots of clothes. They were beautiful but they weren't kind. The youngest daughter was beautiful and kind. Her name was Beauty.

One day, the man said: 'I've got to go to the city. Would you like some presents?'
The older daughters wanted new dresses.
Beauty said: 'I would like a rose.'

What would you like?
Tell a friend.

In the city, the man bought dresses for his older daughters, but he didn't find a rose for Beauty. On the way home, he went through a big forest. Evening came and the man was tired. He saw a castle. The door was open and the man went in. In the dining room, the man saw a fire and a table with lots of food. He was hungry, so he ate the food. Then he went to sleep by the fire.

In the morning, the man went into the garden and he saw lots of flowers.
'I must find a rose for Beauty,' he said.
He found a beautiful pink rose and he picked it. Then he heard a roar behind him.
He turned and saw a big, ugly beast.
'Why are you picking my rose?' shouted the beast.
'It's a present for my daughter,' said the man.
'You can give the rose to your daughter,' said the beast.
'But she must come here and live with me.'

With a friend pretend you are the beast and the man. Act.

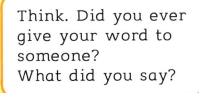

Think. Did you ever give your word to someone?
What did you say?

At home with his daughters, the man didn't talk about the beast. He was sad because he loved Beauty.

'She mustn't go and live with the beast,' he thought. 'She must stay here.'

After a few days, Beauty asked her father: 'Why are you sad?' So her father told her about the beast and the castle.

'I must go and live in the castle with the beast,' said Beauty. 'You gave him your word.'

So the man took Beauty to the castle.

The beast was kind to Beauty.
He gave her beautiful clothes and lots of roses.
Every evening, Beauty had dinner with the beast.
They talked and read stories and were happy.
Beauty often talked about her father and her
sisters. One evening, the beast gave Beauty
a mirror. 'It's a magic mirror,' said the beast.
'You can look in this mirror and see your father
and your sisters.'

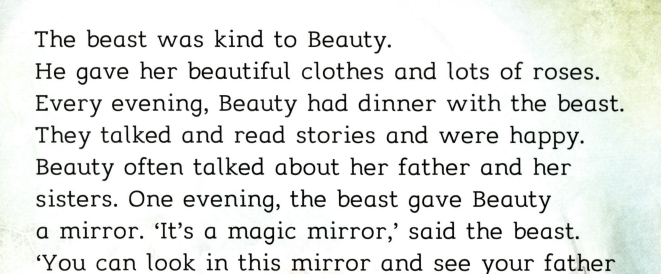

You have a magic mirror. What can you see? Tell a friend.

One day, Beauty looked in the magic mirror and she saw her father. He was ill.
'I must help him,' thought Beauty.
That evening Beauty said to the beast:
'My father is ill. Please can I go home?'
'You can go home for one week,' said the beast. 'Then you must come back.
Take the magic mirror so you can see me sometimes.'

Who does Beauty's father live with?

Beauty went home and helped her father. She put flowers in his bedroom and gave him good food. After a week, he was better. Beauty liked being at home. She stayed for one week, two weeks, three weeks...
She didn't think about the beast. She never looked in the magic mirror. She was happy with her father and her sisters.

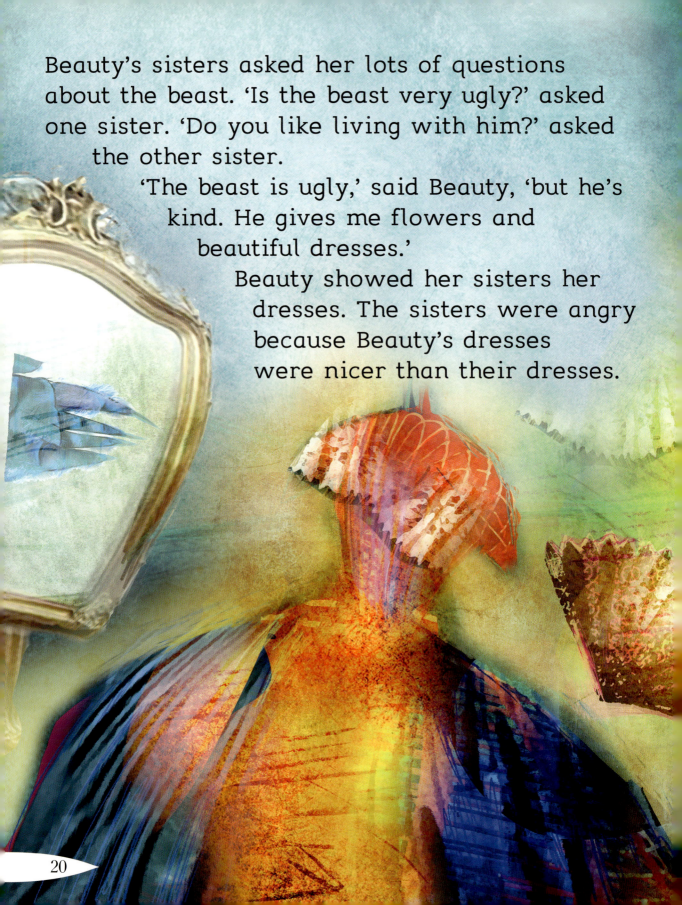

Beauty's sisters asked her lots of questions about the beast. 'Is the beast very ugly?' asked one sister. 'Do you like living with him?' asked the other sister.

'The beast is ugly,' said Beauty, 'but he's kind. He gives me flowers and beautiful dresses.'

Beauty showed her sisters her dresses. The sisters were angry because Beauty's dresses were nicer than their dresses.

One night, Beauty thought about the beast.
'I would like to see him again,' she said.
She looked in the magic mirror and she saw the beast. He was in his garden by the roses. He was sad and ill.
'I must go to the beast now,' said Beauty.
Beauty took her father's horse and rode to the castle.

Think. Why is the beast ill?

Beauty found the beast in the garden and took his hand. The beast looked at her.
'I waited for three weeks,' he said, 'but you didn't come. You don't like me.'
'Yes, I do,' said Beauty. 'I love you.'
There was a flash of light. The beast wasn't ugly now. He was a handsome prince.

The prince told Beauty his story.
'A bad fairy used her magic on me and I became an ugly beast. But you gave me your love, and now I am better. Please marry me, Beauty.'
'Yes!' said Beauty to her prince.

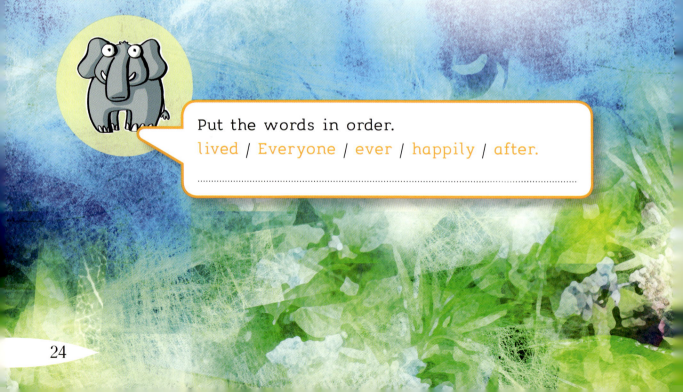

Put the words in order.
lived / Everyone / ever / happily / after.

Play Station 2

1 Look, read and put in the right order.

Beauty went and lived with the beast in his castle.

A man had three daughters. He came to a castle.

The man picked a rose, then he saw an ugly beast.

The beast was sad because Beauty didn't come back.

When Beauty said, 'I love you,' the beast was a prince.

Beauty went home because her father was ill.

2 Look and tell the story to a friend.

26

 3 **Complete the sentences with the correct verbs.**

found
gave
lived
saw
told
turned
went
were

A Beauty .... with her father and her two sisters.
B Beauty's father .... a rose for Beauty.
C Beauty's father .... and saw an ugly beast.
D Beauty .... and lived with the beast.
E The beast .... Beauty a magic mirror.
F Beauty .... her father in the magic mirror.
G Beauty's dresses .... nicer than her sisters' dresses.
H The prince .... Beauty his story.

4 **Find 15 words from the story (→↓). The remaining letters spell the word for a family member.**

```
P D A C A S T L E
R H U N G R Y L U
E F A I R Y G O H
S L R C I T Y V P
E A O R O S E E R
N S A T F I R E I
T H R B E A S T N
A N G R Y I L L C
F O R E S T E R E
```

What do the remaining letters spell?

_ _ _ _ _ _ _ _

27

Play Station 2

 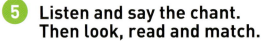

**Listen and say the chant.
Then look, read and match.**

A Why are you picking my rose?
Why are you picking my rose?
The beast is angry – very angry.
Why are you picking my rose?

B I must go and live in the castle.
I must go and live in the castle.
Beauty is sad – very sad.
I must go and live in the castle.

C Her dresses are nicer than ours.
Her dresses are nicer than ours.
The sisters are angry – very angry.
Her dresses are nicer than ours.

D I was ill, but now I'm better.
I was ill, but now I'm better.
The prince is happy – very happy.
I was ill, but now I'm better.

28

6 Read and match.

A Beauty wants a rose. ◯ 'I must go to the beast.'

B Beauty's father gives his word. ◯ 'I must go home.'

C Beauty's father is ill. ◯ 'I must find a rose for Beauty.'

D The beast is sad and ill. ◯ 'I must go and live in the castle.'

  7 Look, read and circle.

Castle rules

- Castle doors close at midnight
- Eat food in dining room only
- Keep out of the garden
- Do not pick the roses
- NO bad fairies

A You mustn't pick the roses. YES NO

B You mustn't eat in the dining room. YES NO

C You must arrive at the castle before midnight. YES NO

D Bad fairies are welcome. YES NO

E You mustn't go into the garden. YES NO

29

Play Station 2

8 Read and match the questions and the answers.

A How many sisters has Beauty got?

B What presents does Beauty's father buy for her sisters?

C Where does the beast live?

D Why is the beast angry with Beauty's father?

E Who gives Beauty a magic mirror?

questions

- - - - - - - - - - - -

answers

New dresses.

Two.

In a castle in the forest.

Because he picks a rose in the beast's garden.

The beast.

9 Think of another question. Ask and answer with a friend.

10 Read and (circle) the speaker.

A Would you like some presents?

B I would like a rose.

C You can go home for a week. Then you must come back.

D Is the beast very ugly?

E A bad fairy used her magic on me.

Play Station Project

Drama

Perform the play of *Beauty and the Beast*.

You need:

The playscript from the internet

Costumes

A mask for the beast

Table and chairs

Some roses

A mirror

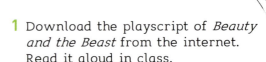

1 Download the playscript of *Beauty and the Beast* from the internet. Read it aloud in class.

2 Decide who is going to play each part. Help each other to learn your lines.

3 Find costumes. Make a mask for the beast. Collect furniture and props.

4 Practise each scene many times.

5 Decide when you are going to perform the play. Make tickets, posters and programmes. Invite your friends and family to the play.

6 Perform the play.

BEAUTY AND THE BEAST

Performed by Class 5

Friday at 3 o'clock

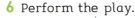

Go to www.helblingyoungreaders.com to download this page.